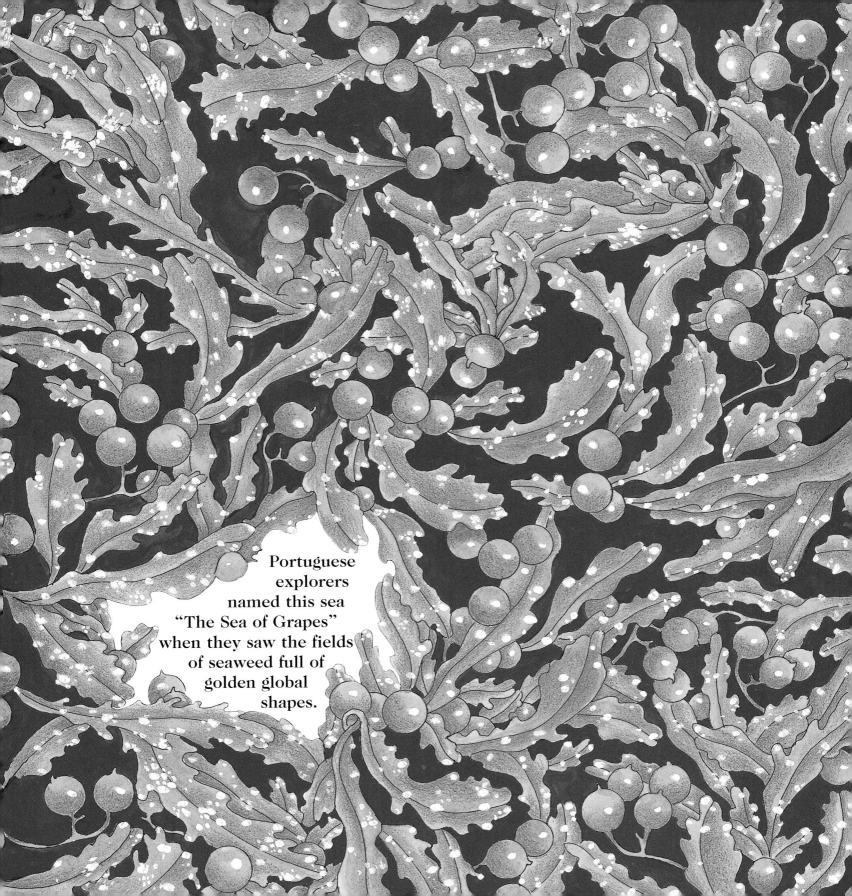

Portuguese
explorers
named this sea
"The Sea of Grapes"
when they saw the fields
of seaweed full of
golden global
shapes.

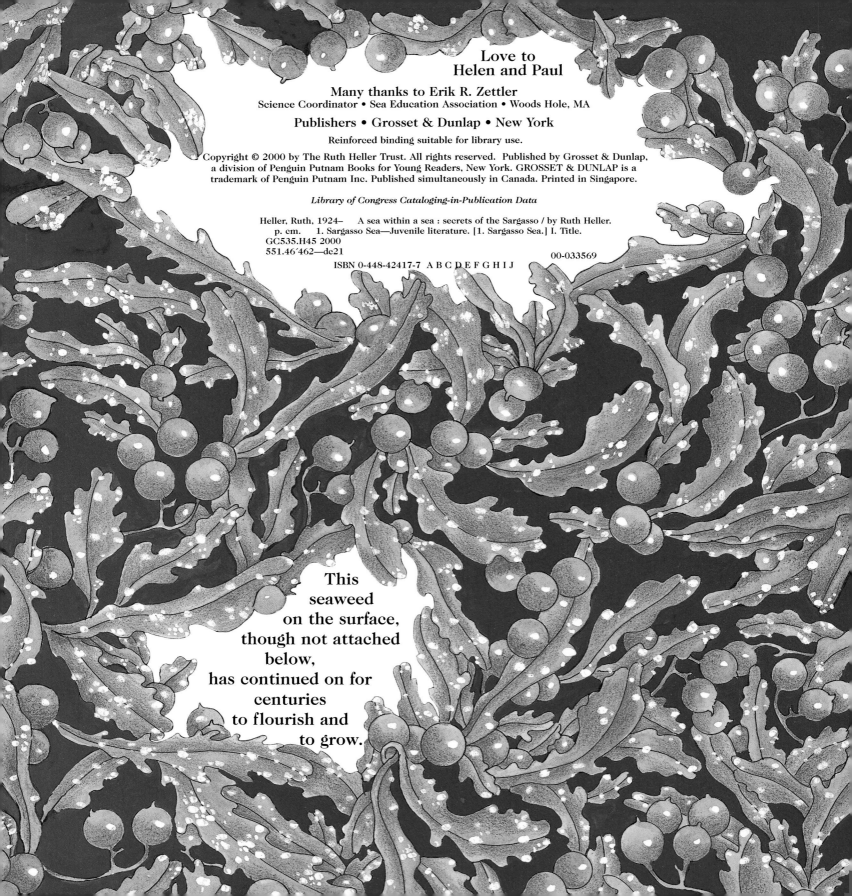

Love to
Helen and Paul

Many thanks to Erik R. Zettler
Science Coordinator • Sea Education Association • Woods Hole, MA

Publishers • Grosset & Dunlap • New York
Reinforced binding suitable for library use.

Library of Congress Cataloging-in-Publication Data

Heller, Ruth, 1924–   A sea within a sea : secrets of the Sargasso / by Ruth Heller.
    p. cm.   1. Sargasso Sea—Juvenile literature. [1. Sargasso Sea.] I. Title.
GC535.H45 2000
551.46´462—dc21   00-033569

ISBN 0-448-42417-7 A B C D E F G H I J

This
seaweed
on the surface,
though not attached
below,
has continued on for
centuries
to flourish and
to grow.

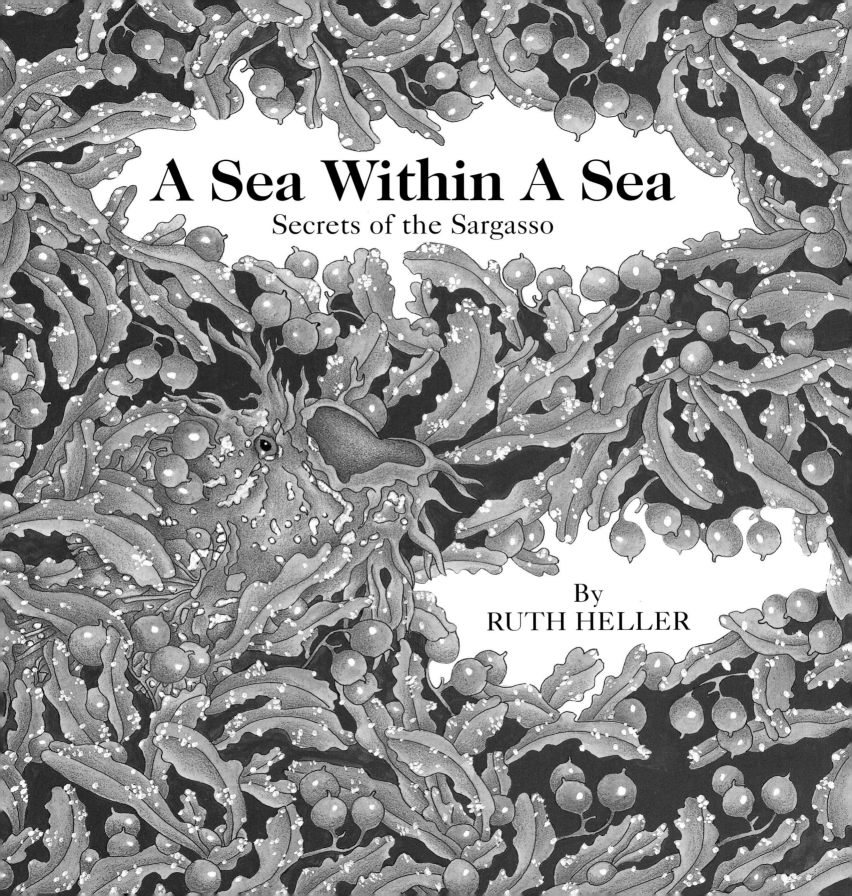

A Sea Within A Sea
Secrets of the Sargasso

By
RUTH HELLER

The mysterious Sargasso
is a sea to dread and fear,
a sea where ships become becalmed
and then they disappear.

There is no land around it.
It's a sea within a sea in the northern cold Atlantic.
It's as warm as tepid tea.

North Atlantic Ocean

It's a whirlpool in slow motion.
It's a sea within an ocean
where
rafts of tangled seaweed
abundantly appear.

It's enclosed
by swirling currents
but
it's calm
and
crystal clear.

Fearsome
are the
legends
of
monsters
huge
and
bold...

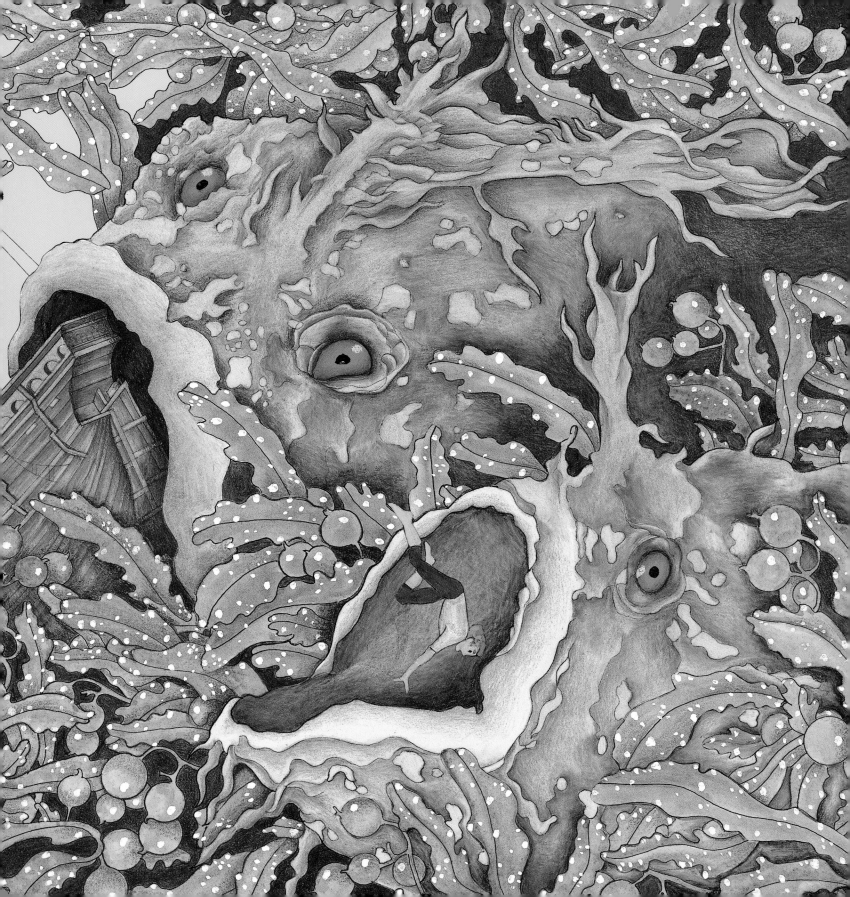

monsters that are hideous
and
gruesome to behold...

and of ships ensnarled forever
in the seaweed's grasping fold...

or doomed
to drift in circles
in the "twilight zone" below
according to the rumors
of many years ago.

But the legends and the rumors are not exactly true.

Columbus met no monsters
in
1492.
His ships became becalmed there,
but
when the breezes blew,
the seaweed was no problem
and
he
bravely
sailed
on
through.

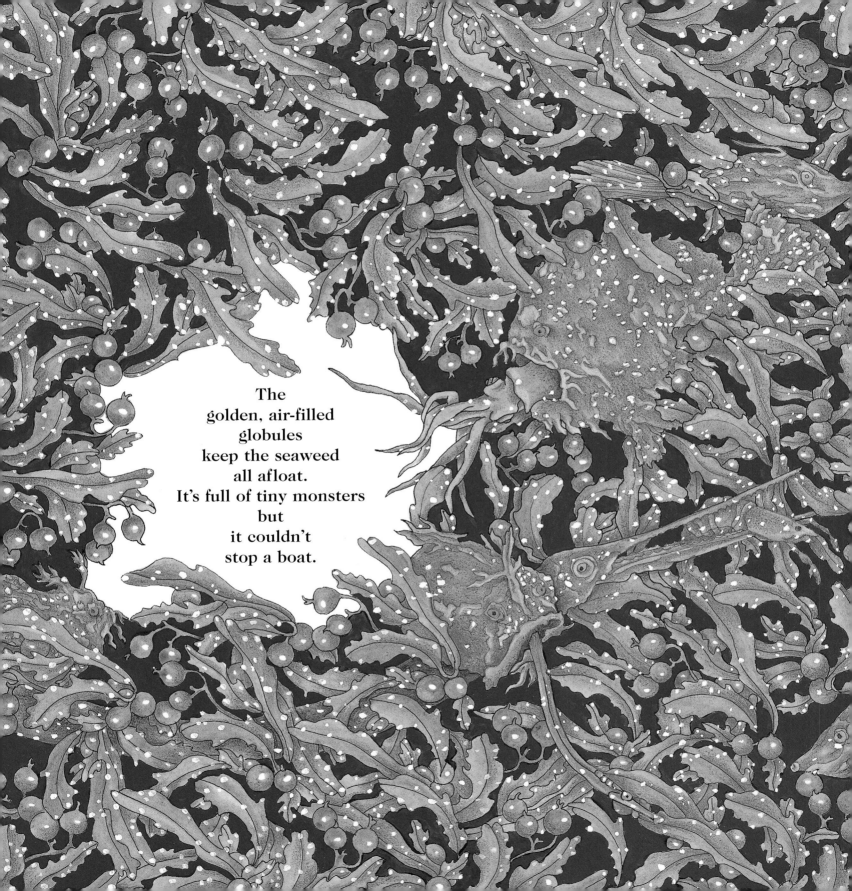

The
golden, air-filled
globules
keep the seaweed
all afloat.
It's full of tiny monsters
but
it couldn't
stop a boat.

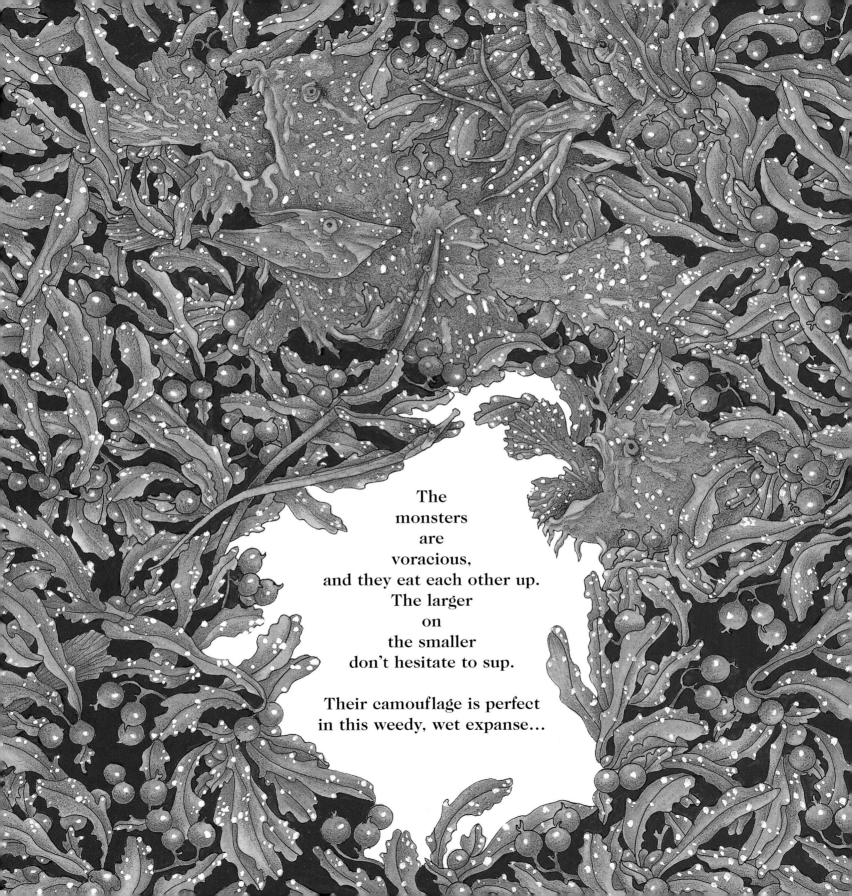

The
monsters
are
voracious,
and they eat each other up.
The larger
on
the smaller
don't hesitate to sup.

Their camouflage is perfect
in this weedy, wet expanse…

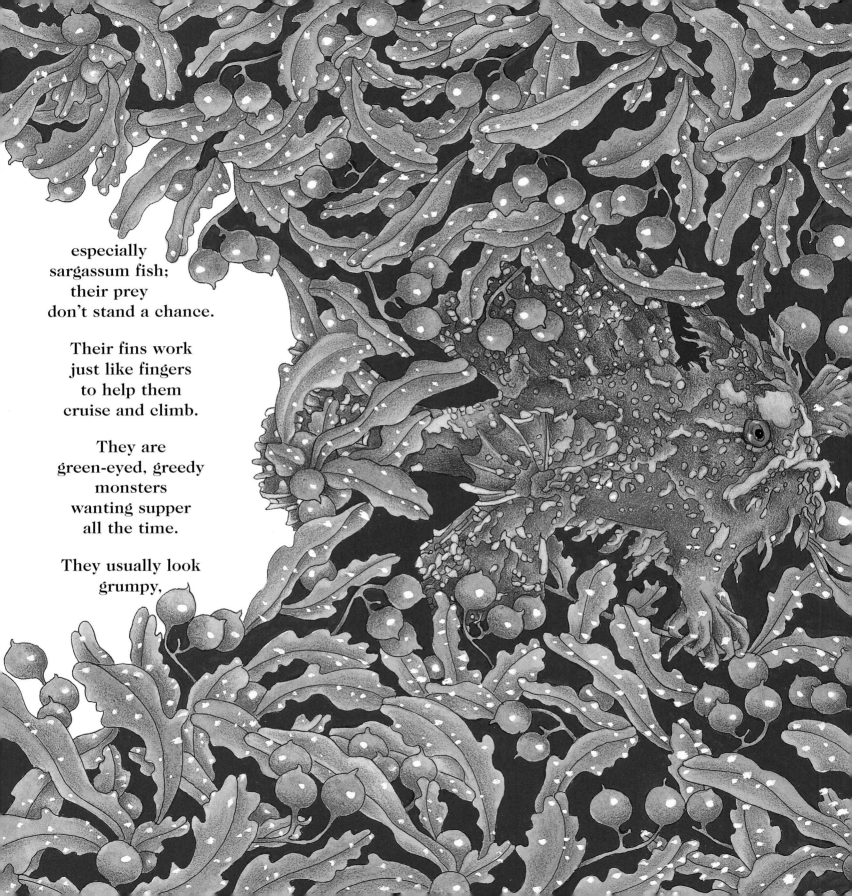

especially
sargassum fish;
their prey
don't stand a chance.

Their fins work
just like fingers
to help them
cruise and climb.

They are
green-eyed, greedy
monsters
wanting supper
all the time.

They usually look
grumpy,

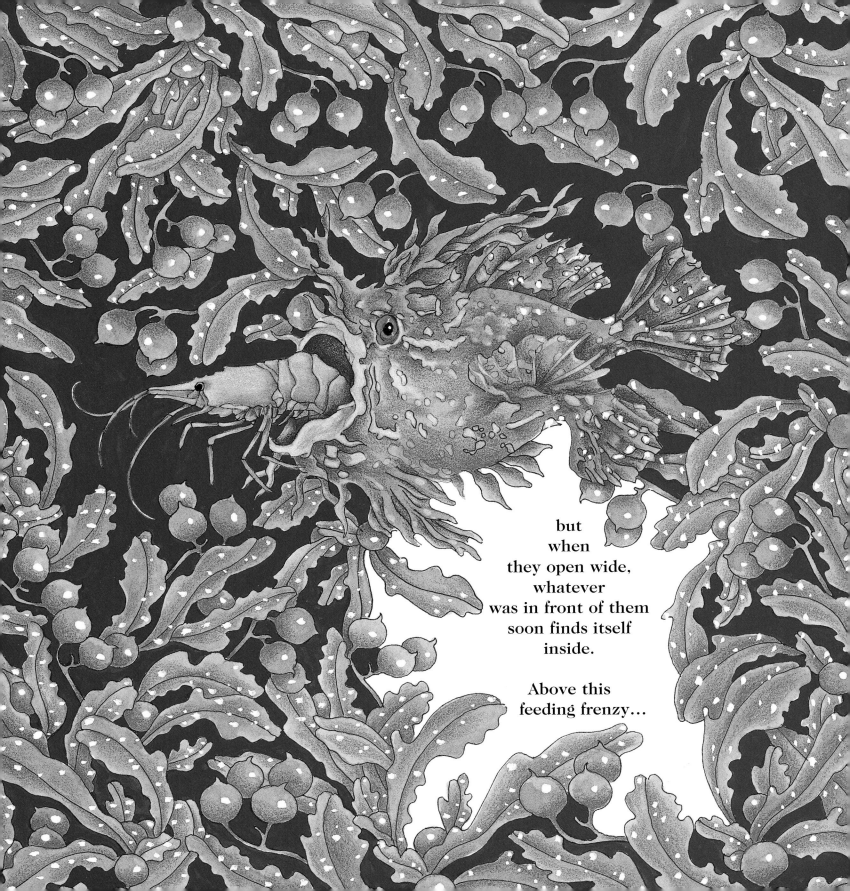

but
when
they open wide,
whatever
was in front of them
soon finds itself
inside.

Above this
feeding frenzy…

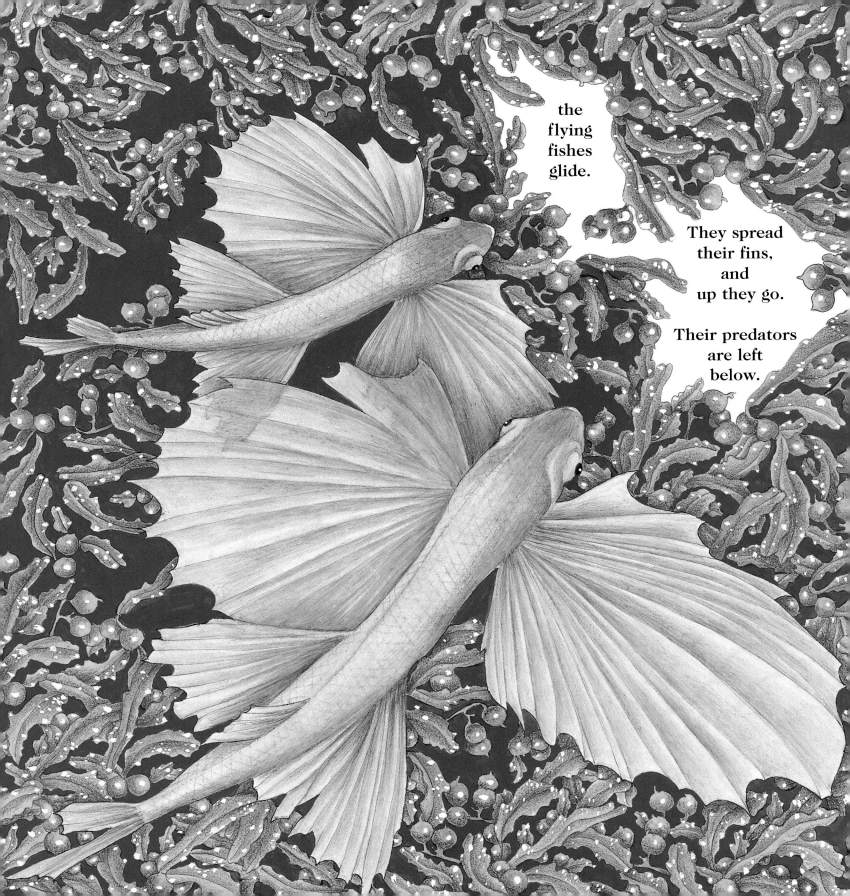

the
flying
fishes
glide.

They spread
their fins,
and
up they go.

Their predators
are left
below.

And
on the
clear
blue
surface
where
the
seaweed
isn't found,
translucent
purple
men-o'-war
and
jellyfish
abound.

Turtles
from
the
zone below
find
them all
delicious.

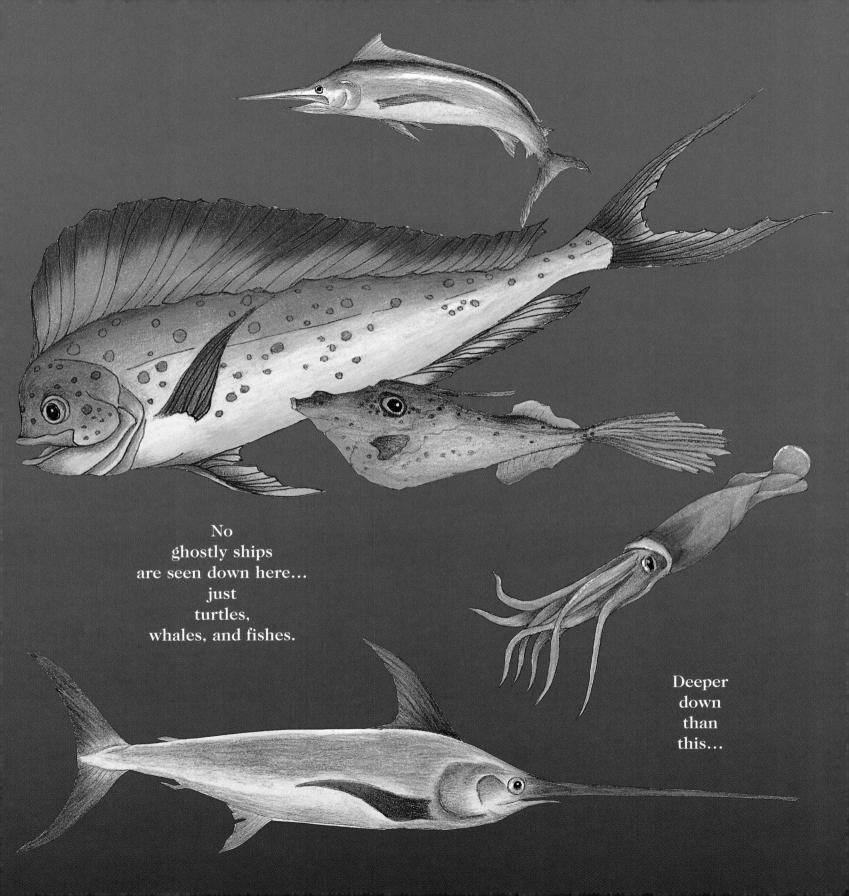

No
ghostly ships
are seen down here…
just
turtles,
whales, and fishes.

Deeper
down
than
this…

in an icy black abyss,
are miniatures of monsters
that provide the only light.

They have fierce, fantastic faces.
They gulp everything in sight.

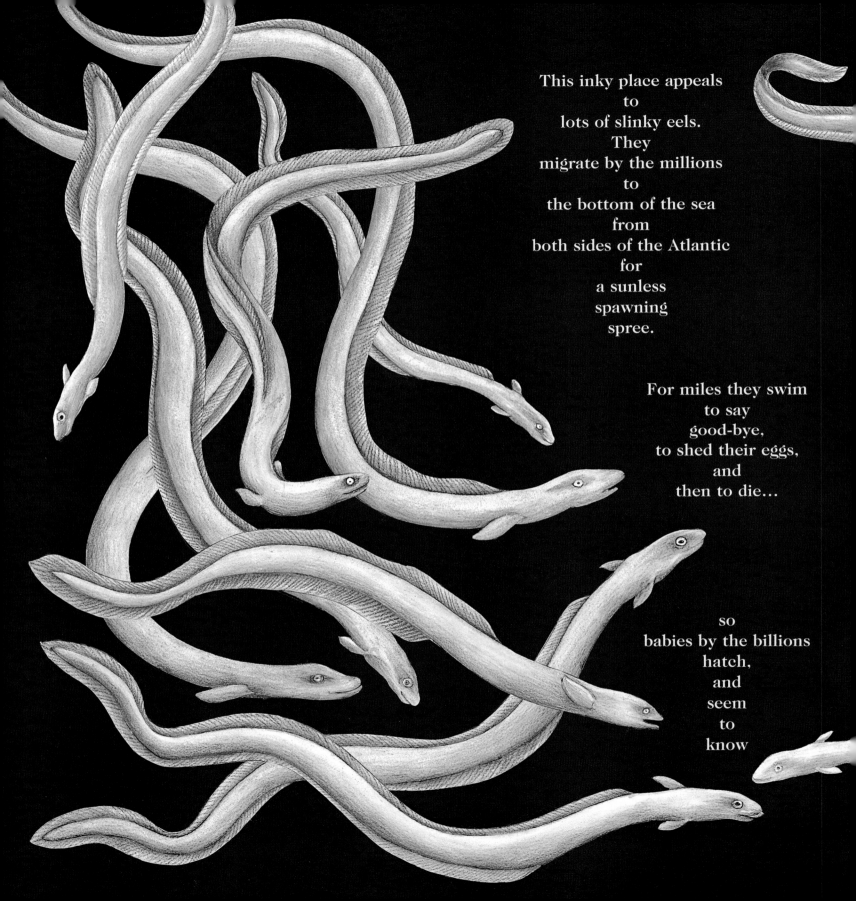

This inky place appeals
to
lots of slinky eels.
They
migrate by the millions
to
the bottom of the sea
from
both sides of the Atlantic
for
a sunless
spawning
spree.

For miles they swim
to say
good-bye,
to shed their eggs,
and
then to die...

so
babies by the billions
hatch,
and
seem
to
know

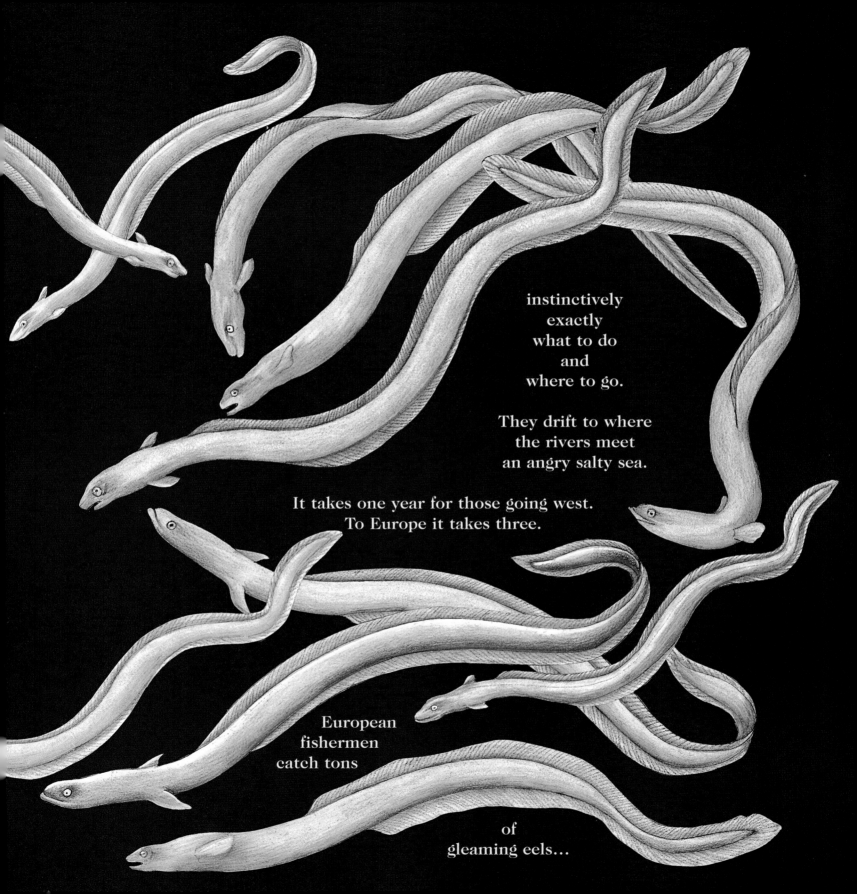

instinctively
exactly
what to do
and
where to go.

They drift to where
the rivers meet
an angry salty sea.

It takes one year for those going west.
To Europe it takes three.

European
fishermen
catch tons

of
gleaming eels…

whose fate it is to
then become
delicious gourmet meals.

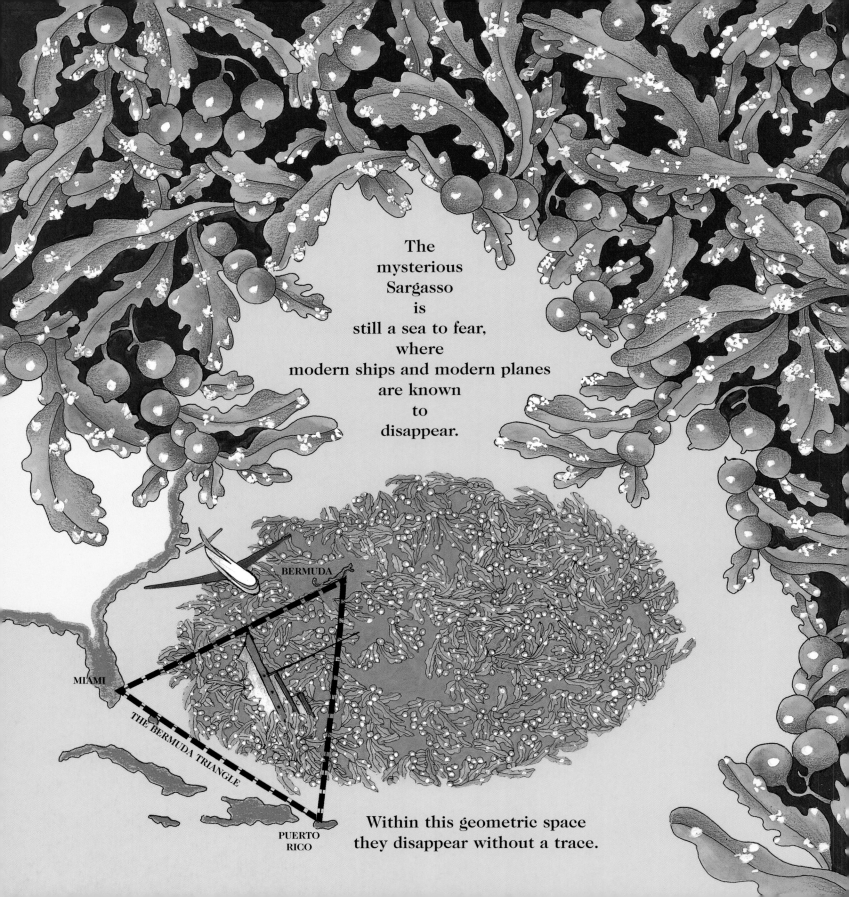

The
mysterious
Sargasso
is
still a sea to fear,
where
modern ships and modern planes
are known
to
disappear.

BERMUDA

MIAMI

THE BERMUDA TRIANGLE

PUERTO
RICO

Within this geometric space
they disappear without a trace.